Samuel French Acting Edition

Mala Hierba

by Tanya Saracho

ıl**SAMUE**

SAMUELFRENCH.C

D0814371

FOR PRODUCTION ENQUIRIES

UNITED STATES AND CANADA

Info@SamuelFrench.com
1-866-598-8449

UNITED KINGDOM AND EUROPE

Plays@SamuelFrench.co.uk
020-7255-4302

Each title is subject to availability from Samuel French, depending upon country of performance. Please be aware that *MALA HIERBA* may not be licensed by Samuel French in your territory. Professional and amateur producers should contact the nearest Samuel French office or licensing partner to verify availability.

MUSIC USE NOTE

Licensees are solely responsible for obtaining formal written permission from copyright owners to use copyrighted music in the performance of this play and are strongly cautioned to do so. If no such permission is obtained by the licensee, then the licensee must use only original music that the licensee owns and controls. Licensees are solely responsible and liable for all music clearances and shall indemnify the copyright owners of the play(s) and their licensing agent, Samuel French, against any costs, expenses, losses and liabilities arising from the use of music by licensees. Please contact the appropriate music licensing authority in your territory for the rights to any incidental music.

IMPORTANT BILLING AND CREDIT REQUIREMENTS

If you have obtained performance rights to this title, please refer to your licensing agreement for important billing and credit requirements.

MALA HIERBA premiered at Second Stage Uptown at the McGinn/ Cazale Theatre in New York City on July 28, 2014. The performance was directed by Jerry Ruiz, with sets by Raul Abrego, costumes by Carisa Kelly, lights by Jennifer Schiever, and sound by Jill BC Du Boff. The cast was as follows:

LILIANA	Marta Milans
MARITZA	Roberta Colindrez
YUYA	Sandra Marquez
FABIOLA	Ana Nogueira

CHARACTERS

LILIANA – Late twenties/early thirties. Wife of border magnate. Always decked out; always impeccable. This is the trophiest of "trophy wives." Lili's got that kind of charm that can't be taught. She was born in Mexico to a proper Mexican family.

MARITZA – Same age as Liliana. Mari is a visual artist based in Chicago, with South Texas roots. Her friends in the lesbian community might call her a "boi" or a "stud," and she wouldn't mind it. She has a few tattoos she loves, some she regrets. She loves fiercely and is fiercely loyal.

YUYA – Older than Liliana by at least twelve or fifteen years, but perhaps older. Yuya raised Liliana and her siblings, and served that household until she imported herself to Liliana's new household when she married. Yuya is usually smarter than anyone in the room, but she hides her resentment well. Hey, she knows her place.

FABIOLA – The very entitled twenty-five-year-old fresa daughter of Liliana's husband. This girl has always had everything and has seldom been told "no."

SETTING

Sharyland, Texas in the Rio Grande Valley

TIME

The span of one week, late this spring

AUTHOR'S NOTES

Overlapping is very important – these women talk like people talk: over one another. Every "/" cues the following line of dialogue. Please adhere to this.

Also: [This denotes the translated Spanish.] Not meant to be spoken.

Scene One

(Thursday Morning: The Cantu's master bedroom. This is a decadent room, with a big wooden bed and matching bedroom furniture. One-thousand-thread-count sheets, that sort of thing. The best that money can buy and also the tackiest money can buy. Alright, not tacky, but these people had Versace furniture back when it was in style, knowhatImean? It's just too much, too fabulous. This house could definitely be on MTV's Cribs. *Lots of creme colors and lots of wood. Gilded things.)*

(The bed is unmade, and it's seen some major action: the sheets are all rumpled and disheveled, and there are belts everywhere. Like, seven of them, strewn across the floor and the bed. Two are fastened to the bed posts as restraints. **LILIANA** *is getting dressed as* **YUYA** *enters.)*

YUYA. A mira pues, I thought you were still in there showering.

LILIANA. Come help me with this.

*(**YUYA** helps zip her up.)*

YUYA. Qué purty, this color. Is this from the big box that came yesterday?

LILIANA. Yes. All the other dresses are disgusting, though. Will you send them all back?

YUYA. Tú y tus Internet addictions. Yeah, I'll send them back. No pero, it does look purty on you, this color.

*(**LILIANA** goes to sit by the vanity and absent-mindedly picks up a belt from the bench and hands it to **YUYA**. The belt is nothing, just a belt. **YUYA***

picks up and puts away belts during the next exchange.)

LILIANA. I also got it in rosita and lilac but both made me look too…Texan.

YUYA. Oooh, lilac would look purty with your green eyes.

LILIANA. Maybe I'll keep that one.

(A crash is heard in the garden. Your general metal-chairs-on-table crash.)

¡Puta madre, Yuya! All morning these men have been / with the banging and the –

YUYA. They're just unloading the chairs and the tables. I just went to supervise. It's fine. / Qué quieres que te diga, it's going to be noisy like that.

LILIANA. Pero qué relajo se traen!

YUYA. It's looking real good down there though. You'll see right now when you go down.

LILIANA. It better look amazing. It better look like a pinche editorial in a pinche magazine with all the money I'm spending.

YUYA. It will, todo mundo will be talking about it. You'll see.

LILIANA. Oh, God I hope so.

YUYA. This room es todo un desmother. I'm going to change these sheets, okay ei? Should I put on the satin ones that he likes?

LILIANA. Ay, no Yuya. Those make me feel so *Scarface*.

YUYA. The peach ones then.

LILIANA. Which peach? Oh, the creme? Sí, pon esas Yuya. *[Yes, put those on, Yuya.]*

(YUYA goes about redressing the bed.)

YUYA. Adivina *[Guess]* who came last night?

LILIANA. Por favor, ¿crees que no me di cuenta? *[Please, you think I didn't notice?]* The whole neighborhood heard her come in in the middle of the night. Driving in like a maniac, stomping around like a pinche elephant.

YUYA. Es una malcriada. *[She is a brat.]*

LILIANA. I don't want to say anything because you know, because I feel bad for her, raised by mother after mother.

YUYA. Please. I have kids okay ei? And they only turned out to be good kids because I gave them sus buenos guamazos *[beat them upside the head]* if they ever got sassy with me. Which is exactly what this girl was missing. With kids you can't be afraid to make a fist.

LILIANA. No, if I ever have kids, I'm never going to hit them. If I ever have kids voy a razonar con ellos. *[I am going to reason with them.]*

YUYA. Yeah, razonar like this with them.

(Makes a bitch slap movement.)

No te digo, *[I'm telling you,]* that's the only way. If not you'll turn out big brats like this one.

LILIANA. Me da lastima. *[I feel bad for her.]*

YUYA. You feel bad for that brat?

LILIANA. A little.

(YUYA continues making the bed.)

YUYA. She didn't never go to sleep. Se fue *[She went]* straight to the study to the computer, she was still up when I get up this morning y viene y me dice en la *[and she comes and tells me in the]* kitchen "I want Eggs Benedict. But with fresh mozzarella instead of ham. Make it." Asi nomas, *[Just like that,]* "Make it." And she never says my name neither, siempre se le olvida. *[she always forgets it]* How long have I worked here and she don't remember my name? Every dog's name she remembers, pero el mío ni maiz paloma. *[but mine, she doesn't remember]*

LILIANA. You know what a big fuss they made when I brought you así que dale las gracias *[so just be grateful]* that she even talks to you. Just don't…

YUYA. Oh, I know. I know. Please, you know that I know how to act. Twelve years working for your family, I know how to act.

LILIANA. I know, just…please, porque va con el cuento con Alberto. *[because she'll go tattle tell to Alberto]*

YUYA. *(To herself.)* "Eggs Benedict"…Pinche huerca.

LILIANA. *(About earrings.)* The gold or the silver?

YUYA. Gold. Aunque the silver looks good too.

LILIANA. I have a million things to do before tomorrow. We have to call the bakery and order a whole new cake. Alberto changed his mind about the red velvet, now he wants tres leches for the party cake. But he still wants it to be five tiers. I can't tell him tres leches doesn't hold up in tiers. It would be mush.

YUYA. Just get him a tres leches para él sólito y dale a *[just for him and give]* everybody else red velvet.

LILIANA. Oh, because it's as simple as that, ¿verdad? You know how he is. He'll check and then, well, we don't want him to get how he gets at his own birthday party. The bakery is going to have to work it out. And I'm sorry that they have a day to make a whole new cake. Pero a ver como le hacen. That is not my problem. Por eso se les paga lo que se les paga, ¿verdad? *[That's why we pay them what we pay them, right?]*

> *(Beat.)*

Santo Dios, que desmadre. *[Dear God, what a mess.]* If his fifty-fifth birthday is this much trouble I don't want to know what will happen when he turns sixty. Me va a dar un infarto. *[I'm going to have a heart attack.]*

YUYA. We'll see if you're around for that.

> *(A dirty look from **LILIANA**.)*

Digo, si Dios nos da vida. *[I mean, God willing.]* You never know what will happen.

LILIANA. No te pases conmigo, cabrona. *[Don't be disrespectful with me.]* You think I don't know what you mean? What people say? I know I'm married to Henry VIII.

> *(She throws a brush at **YUYA**.)*

¿CÓMO ME VAS A DECIR ESO? *[How are you going to say something like that to me?]*

(Consciously quieting down.)

I don't need this shit from you, Yuya! Five years I've lived tiptoeing around this pinche family and I don't need you for eggshells right now. Not you too, pinche cabrona. *[bitch]*

YUYA. I'm sorry. I didn't mean it like that –

LILIANA. Claro que *[Of course]* you meant it like that. Vibora. *[Viper.]*

YUYA. Discúlpame. *[Forgive me.]* I wasn't –

LILIANA. *(Throwing another brush at her.)* ¡Con esa pinche lengua de vibora! *[With that fucking viper tongue!]* You viper!

(FABIOLA enters without knocking.)

FABIOLA. Anybody know if there's an art supply store in this hicksville? I want to paint.

LILIANA. Fabi! ¡Hola muñeca! ¿Llegaste bien? *[Hi. Did you get here okay?]*

(The two kiss on the cheek and FABIOLA throws herself on the freshly made bed.)

FABIOLA. Yeah, sorry I didn't call you guys. I got here like at six actually, but I grabbed dinner with some friends. Did you know there's a P.F. Chang's here now? / Finally, something other than fucking taquerías and Whataburgers. And then we went to this wannabe beer garden place. I'm like, alright McAllen, don't try so hard. But then it was like two a.m. and I was like, fuck, I guess I better get home.

LILIANA. Yes, since last year...

Yuya, eso es todo. Gracias. *[Yuya, that is all. Thank you.]*

(YUYA exits.)

How was the drive?

FABIOLA. What do you mean how was the drive? It was a drive. What am I going to tell you? I drove, I stopped to pee, I ate Cheetos in the car.

(A beat.)

FABIOLA. Can we please talk about the fucking madness going on downstairs? All those men everywhere. I could barely come up the driveway.

LILIANA. They're setting up for your dad's party.

FABIOLA. Obviously. But do they have to be in everybody's way? / Hey, what are you wearing tomorrow. What are you wearing to Dad's thing?

LILIANA. I'm sorry about this Fabi.

>*(She takes a quick beat.)*

Ah, I have a couple of options...

FABIOLA. Can I see?

LILIANA. I don't...do I have them all here? Let me see.

>*(Goes into the closet.)*

FABIOLA. I didn't bring anything that I like and forget trying to find something here. Por favor. I'll end up with a cowboy hat or something...and ropers.

LILIANA. *(Emerging from the closet with two dress bags.)* I was thinking this red one, because it's going to be hot. I don't want to, you know, I don't want to sweat, so no sleeves. But really I think I'm going to wear this white one because I love the –

FABIOLA. Oh, my God. No, you're going to let me wear the white one. Where did you get this?!

LILIANA. I ordered it.

FABIOLA. Where from?

LILIANA. Online.

FABIOLA. From where? I love it!

>*(FABIOLA takes off her clothes to try it on. LILIANA gives a quick sigh. She obviously wanted to wear that one.)*

LILIANA. I don't even remember. You know how you get to shopping online and you have like a thousand opened tabs and you just click buy and...yeah, I don't remember.

FABIOLA. Shuddup, this fits me like a glove. Look at this. Do you have gold shoes?

LILIANA. Aaah, I think so.

FABIOLA. Oh, I really like how it looks. You don't mind do you?

LILIANA. No, como crees. *[No, of course not.]*

FABIOLA. You sure?

LILIANA. Please, no. I was going to wear this red one anyway.

FABIOLA. Okay, great so I got the dress, now for the shoes.

LILIANA. Yeah, let me show you what I got…

FABIOLA. Hey, so you got a new car, huh?

LILIANA. *(Slight "oh no" beat. She knows what's coming.)* … Yeah. You saw it?

FABIOLA. How can one miss it? It's like taking up two spaces in the garage.

LILIANA. Yeah, it's a little ridiculous, isn't it?

FABIOLA. I love it.

　　　　(Pause.)

LILIANA. Yeah, I love it too.

FABIOLA. Yeah.

　　　　(Pause.)

LILIANA. While you're down, if you want to you can drive it.

FABIOLA. Could I?

LILIANA. Of course. It's such a smooth ride.

FABIOLA. I know. I drove it out to get a shake last night.

LILIANA. You what?

FABIOLA. I was dying for a shake, like dying – I'm probably getting my period – and the keys were right there. So I was like, let me check it out. And you're so right, it's like butter. I feel so tall in it. I don't know how easy it can be to have something like that in Houston, like so big, you know? But it's like butter. The seats. Ah, so comfy. And I like all the stuff on the dash.

LILIANA. Yeah, it's like you're driving a spaceship, isn't it?

FABIOLA. I want it.

LILIANA. I have no doubt that – Alberto wouldn't even blink if you asked him for one. How long are you down for? We can go to the dealership together –

FABIOLA. I like that one.

>   *(Pause.)*

I like, totally fell in love with it. The color.

LILIANA. ...ah, my little truck...

FABIOLA. Not so little. Your little...big truck.

>   *(Pause.* **LILIANA***'s trying to deal with the knot in her throat.)*

LILIANA. *(Ah, man, this hurts.)* No.

>   *(Beat.)*

YOUR big truck.

FABIOLA. What? No way.

LILIANA. Yes, please. *Your* truck.

FABIOLA. Are you serious?

LILIANA. Fabiola. Of course. You're the one that's up there in Houston –

FABIOLA. Like for real, for real? You'll give me your car? Title transfer and everything?

LILIANA. Claro. No se diga más. I didn't buy it, right? / You're the one up there working so hard. And studying so hard, you know? Of course. Come on.

FABIOLA. Nope. But your good taste did choose it.
Why are you the best? You are my favorite of my dad's wives, you know that? Totally mean it.

LILIANA. Oh, that means so much to me, Fabi. De verdad. *[For real.]*

FABIOLA. I'm super serious. You know I didn't get along with that gringa he fucking brought back from Arizona. / Ugh. Arizona is the new Alabama, it's a fucking toothless hicksville.

LILIANA. Oh, I know. No, yeah, I know.

FABIOLA. Nasty fucking gringa with no class.

LILIANA. I know.

FABIOLA. I mean it. You're like…you're almost like a sister to me, but like not.

(She pulls out the keys from the pocket of her sweatpants on the bed.)

So, all mine?

LILIANA. Well, we just have to run it by Alberto.

FABIOLA. Oh, I know you'll convince him. You're the best!

(Big hug.)

Oh, and the best taste in clothes. Hands down.

(About the dress.)

Thank you, Lil! It looks good, no?

LILIANA. Way better than it would've looked on me.

FABIOLA. Shuddup, don't say that. I'll give it back to you tomorrow. Okay, I'm going to go get a raspa. That's the one thing I crave from here. In Houston the closest thing we get to it is a slushy but I tell people, I don't want a fucking neon red slushy that tastes like sugary ass, I want a fucking raspa like with the shaved fucking ice from the valley. That's what I want. If I could learn to shave ice myself, I'd totally eat that for breakfast, lunch and dinner.

(Beat.)

Oh, guess who I ran into this morning? Same bright idea, I guess, we were both getting a shake. Maritza Perez. Do you remember her?

LILIANA. Mari Perez?

FABIOLA. Yes! Oh, my God she looks amazing. She was a sore thumb standing there with all her like…I don't know. Gear. She's like all emo or something. Anyway, apparently she was living in Detroit.

LILIANA. Chicago.

FABIOLA. Yeah. Chicago and she's visiting because, actually, I don't know. She told me but I wasn't paying too much attention. Anyway, she's here for a little while. So I invited her to Dad's thing tomorrow.

LILIANA. You what?!

FABIOLA. She's your friend, right?

LILIANA. I haven't talked to her in like decades.

FABIOLA. Oh, she told me she saw you at some wedding? Or a funeral?

LILIANA. I mean, sure. She, she knew my brother and she came down for the memorial but I'm sorry I didn't really talk to her, I literally passed her in the hallway... I didn't really talk to her...

FABIOLA. Well, now you get a chance to catch up.

> (About the dress.)

Hey, thanks again. It fits like a glove.

> (Exiting.)

You know what? I'm going to do something nice for you cuz you've been so badass with me. What flavor raspa do you want?

LILIANA. I don't really...

FABIOLA. Vanilla! I'm going to get you vanilla. So I can have a taste. (Exits.)

> (LILIANA sits down on the bed. The air has been popped out of her chest. Lights go down.)

End of Scene

Scene Two

*(Friday Night: The master bedroom. We hear the
dull sound of a party down below. Clinking and
music and the occasional cackle, etc. You know,
party shit.* **LILIANA** *enters in her red dress. She
looks amazing in it; she's a little sweaty, though.
She digs in a vanity drawer for a packet [not bottle]
of pills from Mexico. Tafil to be exact. She pops one
in her mouth and chases it with the glass of Malbec
she's brought with her. A little while before* **YUYA**
enters with a similar pack.)

YUYA. I couldn't find / your purse.

LILIANA. I found some.

YUYA. Me encontré este paquete *[I found this package]* in the
kitchen. You had another stash behind the diet pills.

LILIANA. Ah, thank God I have foresight. Should I take
two? No porque luego *[No because then]* I'll fall asleep
or something. I don't know what to do? I want to take
the whole freaking box. He hates the band. He hates it.

YUYA. He's over that. He forgot about it as soon as he
yelled at you.

LILIANA. I hope so. I hope he forgot. Osea ojalá because
during the toast all I kept thinking is, chingada madre
[fucking shit] he's going to start yelling as soon as he
sees we couldn't make a five tier tres leches.

YUYA. It's just cake.

LILIANA. Como que *[What do you mean]* it's just cake? It's
not just cake.

YUYA. The governor loved the red velvet. Les dimos tres
pieces. *[We gave him three pieces.]*

LILIANA. I know. It's the only thing that saved me. Did you
see his son? He looks like a movie star now. There was
a time, long time ago, there was a time I thought we'd
end up married.

YUYA. Nombre, *[No way,]* you don't want to move back to Mexico and be a governor's wife. They're killing governors right now. La mafia is making a video game of beheading them for points.

LILIANA. Ay, Yuya! ¿Por qué me traumas? *[Oh, Yuya! Why do you traumatize me?]*

YUYA. Me? The news trauma! They traumatize you every day at six o'clock. People don't even know if what they're watching is the news or some video game con good graphics. Blood everywhere.

    (Beat.)

He did get so handsome though. He got tall. Maybe he won't go into politics like his dad.

LILIANA. Please, they're all politicians. His entire family. There's no way. Let's stop talking about him. If Alberto notices the little looks he's been giving me, no para que quieres… Do I look okay ay?

YUYA. He was watching you like this.

    (YUYA *bugs out her eyes.)*

LILIANA. He was, wasn't he? I'm not just imagining. Good. Oh, but his wife es una mustia. *[is a mousy little thing]* Did you see her? No hips. No boobs. Dark. Ugh. ¿De dónde sacó a esa indita? *[Where did he find that little Indian?]*

YUYA. I didn't believe it was his wife at first.

LILIANA. I know! Yo aquí como que "Hola! Mucho gusto." Guácala. *[Me right here like, "Nice to meet you. Hi." Gross.]*

YUYA. At least the one thing you can say is that you're always the prettiest one everywhere you go.

LILIANA. *(Still messing with her hair.)* At least we can say that.

    (Beat.)

You like my hair like this? Should I wear it down?

YUYA. No, he told you to wear it up. Luego se enoja. *[Then he'll get mad.]*

LILIANA. That's true. But I always feel so old with it up.

YUYA. You don't look old. Se te ve bien. *[It looks good on you.]*

LILIANA. I know, but it makes me feel like I'm thirty-eight or something. Over the hill.

> *(A knock on the door.)*

¿Sí? Adelante. *[Yes? Come in.]*

> *(MARITZA enters the threshold, not the bedroom yet, but her presence is like hot vapor in the room. LILIANA jolts up.)*

Yuya, ve a ver si se ofrece algo abajo. Ándale ve. *[Yuya, go see if someone needs something downstairs. Go.]*

> *(Pause.)*

MARITZA. Hey, Yuya. How you been?

YUYA. *(Ignoring MARITZA, to LILIANA.)* I think maybe you should go downstairs and see if Alberto wants to dance now. Andaba diciendo before that he wanted to dance.

LILIANA. Yuya, go downstairs, I said.

YUYA. I think maybe you should come too.

LILIANA. No te lo vuelvo a repetir! *[I'm not going to say it again!]* Go check on the guests! Go!

> *(YUYA exits, glaring at MARITZA.)*

MARITZA. Bye, Yuya. Nice seeing you too.

> *(Very pregnant pause. Like, nine months pregnant.)*

LILIANA. Hi.

MARITZA. Hi.

> *(Pause.)*

Great party.

LILIANA. Thank you. Been planning it half the year. Did you see who we got to play?

MARITZA. I know. Fancy.

LILIANA. Alberto hated them in person. They sound different in person.

MARITZA. I thought they sounded good. Speakers were a little loud though.

LILIANA. I don't think anyone noticed that. I mean, you know about that sort of thing, but I don't think... people seemed to be enjoying themselves.

MARITZA. They always do at these things, no? All the decadent food and endless drinks.

LILIANA. Let's hope so.

(Pause.)

MARITZA. You look amazing

LILIANA. Thank you. Thanks.

MARITZA. You really do.

LILIANA. Thanks. You look... I like your blazer. It's like eighties, right?

MARITZA. I guess.

LILIANA. Aren't you hot in that? It's too hot for a blazer. ¿No te estás asando? *[Aren't you melting/cooking in it?]*

MARITZA. Alberto's wearing a blazer.

LILIANA. I'm sure he's cooking in it. I'm sure all the men are cooking in their blazers. That's why it's good to be a woman in weather like this, because we can wear things like this and not cook in blazers.

MARITZA. Well, if he can cook in his blazer; I'll cook in my blazer.

LILIANA. I should have gotten giant fans to put everywhere, or cooling stations. *(A pivot.)*

MARITZA. I've been here a week.

LILIANA. Maybe we should go downstairs. Everyone will wonder where I went.

MARITZA. A week, Liliana.

LILIANA. Want to try a fun drink? They designed it just for the party. It's like a mai-tai but better.

MARITZA. I've been sitting on my ass for a whole fucking week asking myself, "Did that phone call really happen?"

LILIANA. I want to go downstairs.

MARITZA. Sitting there at my cousin's, who is too polite to ask, "What the fuck are you doing down here?" And me sitting there wondering the same fucking thing.

LILIANA. Qué malhablada eres, eh. *[What a potty mouth you have, eh.]*

MARITZA. *(Quickly.)* What? See, don't start doing that.

LILIANA. Shut up, I hate it when you act like you don't understand. You speak Spanish.

MARITZA. Since when do I speak Spanish? You won't ever fucking believe that I don't.

LILIANA. Well, why don't you? It's never made sense to me. Your last name is, what it is. Your parents speak it. You look like you do. I mean, it just makes no sense to me.

  (Quick beat.)

Can we please go downstairs?

MARITZA. What am I doing here, Liliana?

LILIANA. I don't know, to be honest. I didn't invite you, not to be rude, but I didn't invite you. So…I don't really know what you're doing here.

MARITZA. Oh, really? You didn't invite me?

LILIANA. Not to the party. No.

MARITZA. Shut the fuck up! What am I doing in Texas?

LILIANA. Could we talk tomorrow? Wait, no because… Could we talk on Monday? I'll meet you at your cousin's on Monday.

MARITZA. You want to wait to fucking talk until Monday?! / I'm supposed to just sit on my ass waiting for you until Monday, when I've been down here for a fucking week with you avoiding my phone calls, just sitting on my ass –

LILIANA. Ssshhhh…sssshhh…calmaditacalmadita…please, Mari. Please.

  (She goes to lock the door.)

Ssshhhh.

MARITZA. I'm not your fucking puppet Liliana.

LILIANA. Por favor no levantes la voz. *[Please don't raise your voice.]* Someone will hear you. This is not how I wanted this to go. / I promise you this is not how I wanted this to go.

MARITZA. And how exactly did you want this to go when I get a phone call in the middle of the night where you sound as if the sky is fucking falling…

LILIANA. No seas exagerada. You take everything so seriously. Sometimes I take an Ambien / and I just get –

MARITZA. Jesus fucking Christ. Are you serious right now?

LILIANA. Listen. Let's go downstairs. Let's just make the best of it and enjoy the party, vale?

MARITZA. This is you on the phone, "Please come down, Mari. You're the only person I can turn to, Mari. Please, please, Mari." You said that – among other things. So my stupid ass gets on the first plane, which is not cheap, Liliana. I get on the first plane because I think, "Fuck, Liliana's about to die or something," and here I am – almost a fucking week because for whatever reason you're now avoiding me and have locked yourself up in your fucking, in your fucking narco compound – do you know how enraging that is? / You ignoring my texts and my Facebooks and my fucking emails?!

LILIANA. Please please keep your voice down.

I'm sorry. You're right. I shouldn't have called you like that in the middle of the… I'm sorry. I promise you, everything is fine. I don't know what I was talking about. Just, just ignore everything I said, okay ay?

(A knock at the door.)

Oh, fuck me. ¿Quién? *[Who is it?]*

FABIOLA. *(Offstage.)* Lili, these shoes suck. I need to look for new ones.

LILIANA. What? Ah, yeah, hold on. *(To* MARITZA.*)* Just… please. Yes, you're right, I owe you an explanation. Tomorrow. Or ah, Monday. I promise.

MARITZA. Fucking puppetmaster.

> (LILIANA *unlocks the door and opens it.* FABIOLA *is a little drunk.)*

FABIOLA. Where the hell did you get these shoes from? They are cheap as hell. The strap is slicing my heel. Only cheap shoes do that. Oh, hey. What are you guys doing in here? What you don't want to be downstairs / dancing to that gadawful…

LILIANA. I was looking for a headache…for an aspirin for Mari, only stronger and we were, you know, catching up.

FABIOLA. Were you?

> *(Taking out some coke.)*

That's nice. It's good to catch up with friends.

> *(To* MARITZA.*)*

You want a bump?

> *(Pause.)*

MARITZA. Sure.

LILIANA. What? Mari, don't. Oh, God.

> *(Goes into the closet.)*

I'll look for some shoes for you. I'll see if I have some shoes.

FABIOLA. Nice hair on her, huh? Hello, prom 1997. Why does she do her hair like that? She tries to so hard. Poor thing.

> *(Bump.)*

Oh, my God. It's so fucking hot out there.

> *(Bump.)*

Let me see your ink.

(MARITZA shows FABIOLA her tattoo. MARITZA bumps.)

FABIOLA. I like that. I like the style cuz it's not too obvious, you know? But it's still a flower. What kind of flower is that?

MARITZA. It's a lily.

FABIOLA. Right. I want like a big arm sleeve tattoo one day. Like from here to here.

MARITZA. Really?

FABIOLA. Not really. But wouldn't that be cool?

MARITZA. Are you the tattoo kind?

FABIOLA. Are you kidding? Look at this.

(She lifts her dress and pulls down her panties.)

It means "bullshit" in Chinese. Or like the equivalent.

MARITZA. Nice.

(LILIANA enters to FABIOLA pulling down her panties. She enters with tons of shoes. She spills them on the table.)

LILIANA. Fabiola, ¿qué haces?

MARITZA. She's showing me her bullshit. Or the equivalent.

(FABIOLA's delighted with MARITZA.)

LILIANA. I brought everything out, everything I think that goes with that dress. I mean, you could do color if you wanted because it's white.

FABIOLA. Maybe I'll just go barefoot. What do you think?

MARITZA. Do it.

FABIOLA. I need a fucking pedicure, though.

MARITZA. Nah.

FABIOLA. Yeah? Barefoot?

(Bump.)

So where did you find that design?

MARITZA. *(Re: tattoo.)* What? This?

FABIOLA. Yeah, who drew it? I might want a flower like that. Like right here.

MARITZA. I drew it.

FABIOLA. You drew that? That's like really good.

MARITZA. Well, thank you.

LILIANA. Maritza is actually an amazing artist, I mean, do you still do your art thing?

MARITZA. Unfortunately. Yeah. I never learned to do something respectable with my life.

LILIANA. She's being modest but she's actually kind of famous, right?

MARITZA. I wouldn't use the term famous.

FABIOLA. Shuddup, are you serious?

MARITZA. Your *stepmother* here is being kind. I have a gallery. And yeah, some people like my work. But I wouldn't say that makes me famous.

FABIOLA. Shuddup, that's amazing. Dude, I paint. I do.

MARITZA. Oh, yeah?

LILIANA. She makes these like, huge canvas things with –

FABIOLA. Shuddup. I love it. Okay, you have to take a look at my stuff.

MARITZA. Sure.

FABIOLA. Lili, who knew that you had cool friends! Like, who knew.

(*Offering coke.*)

Lili?

LILIANA. I don't...no thanks.

FABIOLA. Oh, right. Pills are your thing.

LILIANA. ¿De qué hablas? *[What are you talking about?]*

FABIOLA. I don't blame you, to deal with my dad you need like an IV of Xanax to like drag around with you. My dad, as soon as you start to be emotional about anything – shit you could be watching *Oprah* or like a Disney movie with puppies and who doesn't cry at that, you know? But you start crying and it annoys my dad

so much that he'll literally pop a pill in your mouth.
I mean, like he'll take out a pill, pull down your jaw
and pop the fucking Tafil in your mouth. All those pills
right there? Reynosa. They're all from Mex. He doesn't
need a prescription. He's got everyone sedated with
those fucking pills, right Lili?

LILIANA. Everybody takes those. I only take it here and
there when I'm stressed. Tafil is for children anyway, I
just take the child dose

FABIOLA. Pop two in your mouth: grown up dose. Pop
three:

(Snores.)

This party sucks. The music is atrocious. I told my dad
that that band was shit.

LILIANA. Did you?

FABIOLA. It's shit. Mari, let's go do something. You seem
like a fun girl. Let's go look for trouble in this shithole
of a town. What do you think?

MARITZA. *(Pause.)* Okay. I'm down.

FABIOLA. Awesome.

LILIANA. I don't know if you should... Mari and I were
catching up since...she's leaving tomorrow.

FABIOLA. Are you leaving tomorrow?

MARITZA. Maybe.

FABIOLA. Ah, well if you're leaving then we should
definitely go party, you know?

MARITZA. Like I said...I'm down.

LILIANA. But we didn't get to catch up. We were...we didn't
get to catch up and I haven't talked to you in so long
and we were catching up.

MARITZA. Maybe I'll stay till Monday then. We can catch
up later.

LILIANA. Why don't we catch up now?

FABIOLA. *(Laughing.)* – Sounds like the two of you are
saying you want some ketchup. Like for fries.

(Laughing.)

Come on, let's peace out. Liliana, tell Papi I had to go. That I just had to go because this music, it's making my ears bleed. Okay?

LILIANA. He's going to be angry.

FABIOLA. Well, make sure he's not. You're so good at calming him down.

(To **MARITZA.***)*

I've never seen anyone calm him down the way she does. I don't know what she does. You got like fairy dust. Okay, let's go. Ciao ciao.

*(***FABIOLA*** exits. ***MARITZA*** lingers.)*

Maritza!

MARITZA. Monday.

*(***LILIANA*** looks like a wet dog or something. No air in her chest again. A moment.)*

End of Scene

Scene Three

(Friday into Saturday: The back deck of the Cantu's huge patio. There are beautiful equipales with the family crest and lots of fabulous patio décor. It's, like, tacky but fabulous, you know? Firstly with a touch of Northern Mexico, including some Tapatío pieces [like the equipales and some big talavera vases] but also with a little Southwest/ American comfort thrown in there, like stuff from the Sharper Image. There's one of those electronic, self-contained fire pits, and the wavy light from the pool reflects onto the deck, giving it a sort of glow. LILIANA is sitting in the dark, although it's not that dark since the pool is lit and the Texas moon is smiling. She's eating a bowl of Fritos with lime juice and salsa Tabasco. She licks her fingers every so often. Maybe she uses an exprimidor de limones to put more lime on the Fritos. She's got the cordless house phone and her cell phone, which she checks a couple of times. It's like three or four a.m. Dude, it's mad late. She should be in bed. YUYA enters after a while.)

YUYA. That's gonna put a big hole in your stomach.

LILIANA. This is my second bowl.

YUYA. Shoot, I'm going to have to roll you up the stairs.

LILIANA. Shut up Yuya. Fuck, why don't I smoke? If I smoked I'd be super skinny.

YUYA. Maybe you should take it up. No porque luego the man upstairs, he wouldn't like the smell.

LILIANA. ¿Verdad? My hair would reek. Okay, we need a better plan to make this little belly be flat again. It needs to go down like this, not stick out like that. Guácala, I'm so gross.

YUYA. I didn't want to say it, but you are getting a little wide right here in the middle.

LILIANA. Shut up, don't say that to me Yuya. Are you serious?

YUYA. Have I ever lied to you?

(*Freaked-out pause.*)

LILIANA. Oh, my God you're right. I think I'm growing some back fat. Do you see? I'm getting back fat and love handles. Qué trauma.

YUYA. The best was when you used to throw up, that's when you look the best.

LILIANA. Yeah, I looked so good then. You could see my bones right here. But my breath smelled so bad and you know… I kept getting dizzy everywhere.

YUYA. Plus your hair…

LILIANA. Oh, I know. I thought I was in that movie *The Craft* all of a sudden. Like that girl washing her hair in the school shower and she's like washing it and it's coming off all over her hands. Cállate, no me lo recuerdes. *[Shut up, don't remind me of it.]* Imagine if I lost my hair? I'd be so ugly.

(**YUYA** *nods in agreement. A quick moment.*)

Maybe we need to go back to Monterrey for those injections again because that totally worked. I was so skinny with the injections because I couldn't keep anything down. But we need to find a doctor who doesn't make me break out into hives. I don't know what was in that stuff, but the last time we went –

YUYA. Uy, you looked like the Swamp Thing.

LILIANA. I did. Shut up, Yuya. Stop stressing me out.

(*Eats more Fritos.*)

¿Ya ves cómo me tienes? *[You see how you have me?]* Here I am eating trash. But why does it have to be so fucking good?

YUYA. You gonna rot your guts.

LILIANA. Good, maybe I'll get an ulcer and not get hungry.

YUYA. Luego *[Then]* you're gonna be complaining in the morning that acid reflux this and que acid reflux that.

LILIANA. What are you talking about, it is morning. It's going to be light out in a couple of hours.

(*Beat.*)

Ah, I hate it when Fabiola's here. I fucking hate it when she comes down. Right when we got Alberto calm and…you know, appeased and mansito, aquí vienes esta pinche huerca… *[tame, here comes this fucking…]*

(*Beat.*)

I'm going to have to give her the car, you know? Hija de su puta madre. *[Motherfucker.]* I'm going to have to give her my fucking truck.

YUYA. I don't know. Her daddy no está muy happy with her. *[is not very happy with her]*

LILIANA. Oh, please. He always does whatever she wants in the end. Always gets her way. Nada más saca la mano. *[She just sticks out her hand.]*

(*Stretching out her hand.*)

"Please, Papi. Papito por favor." *[Daddy, please.]*

(*Beat.*)

Wait.

(*Goes to look through the glass door.*)

Imagínate si nos cacha Alberto. Por favor Diosito que no se despierte. *[Imagine if Alberto catches us. Please God don't let him wake up.]* We're all fucked if he wakes up and sees his Porsche missing. How did she find the keys? I don't even know where he keeps the fucking keys. Me lleva… *[Fuck me…]*

YUYA. ¿Para que te preocupas por ella? *[Why do you worry about her?]*

LILIANA. ¿Cómo qué por qué me preocupo? *[What do you mean why do I worry?]*

YUYA. I don't understand why you're sitting out here todo worried about her.

LILIANA. She's got his car, Yuya. ¿Estás mensa? *[Are you stupid?]* She's got his car.

YUYA. Alla ella, that's her problem.

LILIANA. *(Raising her voice, then catching herself.)* It's everybody's problem. He wakes up and notices that she's gone with his brand new – I mean, the man hasn't even gotten to drive it, we went around the neighborhood for ten minutes.

YUYA. He took you to the beach in it.

LILIANA. Well, yes, he took me to the beach in it. Still.

YUYA. You're not mad because she took his car, tú 'tas enchilada cuz she went off with Maritza, to who knows where.

LILIANA. Yuya.

YUYA. Am I saying the truth here?

LILIANA. Mejor te callas Yuya.

YUYA. You are out here in the middle of the night waiting because you can't stand that / your little friend there…

LILIANA. I'm going to throw this bottle at you / let it splatter and hit you with hot sauce in the eye!

YUYA. Ándale. *[Go on.]* Throw it and wake him up.

> *(LILIANA puts the bottle down. Glares at YUYA. Silence.)*

YUYA. You think I say this to make you mad or something.

LILIANA. I know you say it to make me mad.

YUYA. Lili, if he ever gets wind of –

> *(In a flash LILIANA has gotten up and is holding YUYA by the face. Tight. One hand on her throat maybe. This shuts YUYA up. For a moment.)*

LILIANA. Shut up! Cierras el hocico or do I shut it for you?!

> *(Pause.)*

YUYA. He'll kill you.

LILIANA. I know he will.

>   *(Pause.)*

YUYA. You think I don't have feelings and that I don't feel anything and that when we clean you up in the morning from, from whatever he does to you at night –

LILIANA. Te estás pasando, Yuya. *[You're crossing the line, Yuya.]*

YUYA. Hey, I've been married too.

LILIANA. I doubt your husband had my husband's appetite, I doubt it very much.

YUYA. I know. Por eso digo *[That's why I'm saying]* that I'm not just saying this to be some jerk or something. Lili, you're like my daughter. To me you're like a daughter.

LILIANA. I know.

YUYA. You know that's the truth. And my job is to take care of you. When I saw her here, in your house. It's just bad business / to have her here.

LILIANA. Just stop talking, Yuya.

YUYA. I knew there would be trouble. There can be trouble if you don't just, send her away. You need to send her away.

LILIANA. I tried.

YUYA. No. You can't half-ass try. You gotta send her away.

LILIANA. Oh, like I have any power over whether she comes or goes. She doesn't listen to me. Nobody listens to me.

>   *(Sound of garage door.)*

The door – the garage door.

>   *(YUYA gets up to go see.)*

Wait, don't go. Wait until she goes upstairs or she goes to get online. I just want to make sure the car is in the garage.

YUYA. She probably left wrappers and things y sabra Dios qué tanto. *[and God knows what]* I'm going to have to go in there and clean it up.

LILIANA. Yeah, we clean it up when she goes to –

YUYA. The keys. We need the keys from her. Si no la jodimos. *[If not we're fucked.]*

> (Suddenly **FABIOLA** *bursts out onto the deck, as she's taking off her top. She's followed by* **MARITZA**.)

FABIOLA. …because they don't fucking trust me with house keys like if I'm nine years old! It's like Gestapo nation up in here.

> (Re: shirt.)

Help me take this off.

> (**MARITZA** *helps her with the shirt.*)

MARITZA. Fabi, I think you should call it a night.

FABIOLA. No, come on, the pool is heated. We'll swim and it'll be so perfect.

> (**FABIOLA** *notices the other women.*)

OhmyGod, what are you two doing here. Like little gargoyles.

> (To **YUYA**.)

Oh, yes perfect, you! Hey! Will you make us some –

> (To **MARITZA**.)

Do you want tuna fish? I am like feenin' for some tuna fish with lots and lots of mayo right now. Like a vat of mayo. Do you want some?

> (To **YUYA**.)

Will you go make us some. Like right now.

> (**YUYA** *gets up to go.*)

YUYA. Do I bring you something to drink?

FABIOLA. Yes, you bring us something to drink. What are we going to eat the sandwiches with nothing to drink? Mari, what do you want to drink?

MARITZA. I'm good. I don't need anything.

FABIOLA. Oooh, freshly squeezed lemonade. With like the whole thing of sugar, pour the whole jar of sugar in there. Con Topochico. Go.

(*YUYA exits.*)

Let's jump in now because we die if we eat and then swim. Isn't that what they say? That you'll get like a cramp in your stomach and die.

MARITZA. Maybe we should chill for a little bit.

FABIOLA. Fuck that, I thought we were going to jump in.

LILIANA. Fabi, maybe you shouldn't. Your dad can wake up.

FABIOLA. Fuck him. He didn't even pay attention to me at the fucking... Did you see how he's treating me?

LILIANA. ¿Qué esperabas? It really hurt him when you left in the middle of his party.

FABIOLA. I came down for him, didn't I? I was there at the fucking party. Oh, God he's such a fucking...

(*About the Fritos.*)

What the hell is this?

MARITZA. It's Fritos with lime and hot sauce.

FABIOLA. That's disgusting.

MARITZA. It's actually really really good.

FABIOLA. No way. Let me taste.

(*Eats.*)

This is like...gross good.

MARITZA. I think um...we have a little situation with the car.

LILIANA. What do you mean with the car?

MARITZA. I think, you're going to have to call a tow truck. But maybe not.

FABIOLA. Oh, it's not even that serious, I just didn't want to figure it out this late –

LILIANA. Where's the car?

MARITZA. That's why I gave her a ride –

LILIANA. Where's the car.

MARITZA. It's at the bar.

FABIOLA. We left it in the parking lot.

LILIANA. What happened to it?

FABIOLA. The freaking tree. There shouldn't be trees in parking lots, it's so fucking stupid. You put a tree in the middle of a parking lot, you're going to run into it when you're backing up. It's like simple geometry.

MARITZA. The headlight got a little beat up –

LILIANA. Backing up?

MARITZA. Sort of. I mean, the left brake light too.

LILIANA. Dios mio, ¿qué va a decir tu Papá?

FABIOLA. Fuck him. It's a fucking car. A fucking obvious-ass Porsche, hello. Can you get any more obvious than that. My dad is so fucking obvious about everything. This fucking house, his fucking cars, his little wives – no offense Lili, you know I adore you, but he's such a fucking douche. You know what's a good classy fucking car? A Bugatti. That's a real fucking car. Have you seen those cars? Have you seen them?

MARITZA. No.

FABIOLA. You would die.

MARITZA. *(To* **LILIANA.***)* I can take it to my cousin's in the morning.

LILIANA. Could you take it to him right now?

MARITZA. I can't wake him up right now.

LILIANA. Could you take it first thing? Alberto leaves for Guadalajara for the whole weekend and he won't be back until Tuesday and if we are lucky he won't notice when Chuy drives him to the airport in the morning.

FABIOLA. You know what? Let's go wake Papi. Papi! I'm going to wake him and tell him that I took it and I rammed it into a tree. Papi! I don't care. Papi!

LILIANA. We don't want to do that, Fabi. De verdad. *[Seriously.]* We have three days to make it right, y qué suerte porque si se entera tu papá que andabas – *[and we're lucky because if your dad finds out that you were –]*

FABIOLA. I don't care. You think I care? Tell him. I'll tell him as soon as he wakes up.

LILIANA. Fabiola!

FABIOLA. Are we going to jump into the pool here?

MARITZA. Not right now, Fabi.

FABIOLA. My buzz is like…

(*Makes "womp womp" sound.*)

How long does it take to make tuna sandwiches for God's sake?

(*Beat.*)

Lili, I love that color on your nails. You're cool, you know that? I like you. Mari, Lili is my favorite of my dad's wives.

MARITZA. Yeah, you said that.

FABIOLA. He's had some bad fucking bad taste, straight up. There's no one like my mom, man. No one like my mom. No offense, Lili. You're like awesome. But some of these…ugh. I hate white people. There. I said it. I hate white people. I would never date a white guy. I mean a white Mexican, sure. But like, a white American? Yuck. Would you date a gringo, Mari? A gringa.

MARITZA. I date all kinds. I take people as they come.

FABIOLA. Yeah, I do too. I mean, yeah. I don't really hate white people. Come on, I live in Houston. How would I hate white people?

(*Beat.*)

I want to visit you in Chicago.

(*Oh, man, sloppy drunk now.*)

I like you, Mari. I like you a lot. I'm coming to Chicago. I'm so coming to see you for sure.

MARITZA. Yeah?

FABIOLA. Yeah.

LILIANA. It's very cold in Chicago. It's like sub-zero in the summer.

MARITZA. Is that why you've never been to Chicago? Because of the temperature? I mean, you've never been to Chicago, have you?

LILIANA. Why would I go to Chicago? There's nothing in Chicago for me. There's nothing…what's there in Chicago? I'd rather go to like, New York, if I'm going to go somewhere freezing cold.

MARITZA. New York is not as cold as Chicago.

LILIANA. Exactly.

FABIOLA. *(About the Fritos plate.)* I want to like, lick this plate.

MARITZA. Told you it was good.

FABIOLA. Fuck Yuya. Why is she taking so long? Am I going to have to carry these sandwiches out myself?

(Exits.)

LILIANA. You want to go follow your girlfriend over there?

(MARITZA smiles big.)

All of a sudden you're BFFs, the two of you? What you could possibly have in common with that girl –

MARITZA. She's actually not bad once you get her to calm the fuck down. She has a lot of potential.

LILIANA. Oh, she has a lot of potential? She has a lot of potential.

MARITZA. Why are you getting all worked up?

LILIANA. I'm not getting all worked up.

MARITZA. I think you're tweaking / out a little bit.

LILIANA. Ugh, I'm going to… I'm going to take this bowl and bust open your head right now. I want to fucking beat you over the head with this.

(MARITZA smiles super big.)

Stop smiling. Stop it. I hate you.

MARITZA. No you don't.

LILIANA. *(Diffused. A beat.)* I do. Te deteste. *(Beat.)* Pinche Mari. How bad is the car?

MARITZA. I mean I'm not going to lie, it's not like he won't notice if you don't get it fixed. There's a big hole in the headlight and the brake light is dangling.

LILIANA. What the hell was she doing? Why was she driving? Why did you let her drive?

MARITZA. Hey, I brought her back in one piece, okay? But I'm not her babysitter. You can't babysit that.

LILIANA. Mari?

MARITZA. Yeah?

LILIANA. I think you should go.

MARITZA. Yeah, I think I should go too. We don't want old boy coming down in his bathrobe finding me here. I think Fabi's okay and she's in your capable hands now. Going to peace out now.

>*(Starting to leave.)*

Lovely seeing you –

LILIANA. No, I mean you should go. Go back home.

MARITZA. You know that's not going to happen until we talk. I've sat around all week waiting for a word from you.

LILIANA. There's nothing to talk about. Everything's actually fine.

MARITZA. I'm not leaving until we have a proper talk. And I promise you, this will be the last time we talk, Liliana. / The last time. Because I'm not doing this shit again!

LILIANA. God. Not here, please. Shhhhh. Keep your voice down, Maritza. Please…

>*(Silence. **MARITZA** stares at **LILIANA**. For, like, a long time. After a while, **YUYA** enters with the tuna sandwiches and the keys to the Porsche.)*

YUYA. She passed out.

>*(Holding out the keys.)*

Are you all still eating the sandwiches?

LILIANA. Nobody's eating sandwiches, Yuya! Here give me these.

(*Grabs keys from* **YUYA**.)

Mari, I'll meet you super early at your cousin's right after Alberto leaves. His flight leaves at eight so he'll be leaving around seven, six thirty. I'll text you when I'm on my way.

MARITZA. I might forget to have my phone on.

LILIANA. Don't joke with me right now, Maritza.

MARITZA. Come on. When have I failed you?

(*Pause.*)

YUYA. (*Picking up* **FABIOLA**'s *t-shirt from the ground.*) I think we should move this girl upstairs before she drools or guacareas en el [barfs on the] sofá.

LILIANA. Yeah, you go take her upstairs, Yuya. I'm walking Mari out.

(**YUYA** *exits with a glare at* **MARITZA**.)

MARITZA. When have I failed you?

(**LILIANA** *grazes* **MARITZA**'s *cheek tenderly as they exit.*)

End of Scene

Scene Four

(Sunday Afternoon: A motel room. **MARITZA** *has just helped* **LILIANA** *onto the dresser as the lights are coming up.* **LILIANA**'s *only wearing a bed sheet around her.* **MARITZA**'s *in front of her in a tank top and boy shorts.)*

MARITZA. *(Re: sheet.)* More over the shoulder.

LILIANA. Like this?

MARITZA. Yeah. Now just stand there for me.

*(***LILIANA*** stands in her pose, then feels silly.)*

LILIANA. *(Starts getting off the dresser.)* Mari, me siento ridícula. *[Mari, I feel ridiculous.]*

MARITZA. No, come on, babe. Just stand for me.

(She's all hands with **LILIANA** *and turns her around.)*

Let me see your back.

LILIANA. Are you arresting me?

MARITZA. No, I'm imagining you with wings.

*(***MARITZA*** runs her hands all over* **LILIANA**, *then she pulls off the sheet.)*

LILIANA. Hey!

MARITZA. Lilith sprouted these amazing wings and dragon talons. All my new pieces are of wings and talons.

LILIANA. I don't want dragon talons.

MARITZA. Oh, but you do. Lilith was a badass with fucking dragon wings. She'd terrorize men in their sleep and incite nocturnal emissions from them.

LILIANA. Her superpower was making guys have wet dreams?

MARITZA. Yeah. And also killing babies. A hundred babies a day. / So some people think of her more as a demon.

LILIANA. What.

Well, yeah. If she went around killing babies.

MARITZA. It's complicated. She only killed the babies because God sent his angels to kill her babies for leaving Adam.

LILIANA. I never heard any of this.

MARITZA. Before Eve, God made Lilith. /

> *(Beat.)*

And God made her equal to Adam in every way. But Adam was kind of an asshole who got it in his head that she should lie beneath him and let him fuck her.

LILIANA. Is this in the Bible?

He liked to do it missionary style. Nothing wrong with that.

MARITZA. No, he didn't want her on top. As in, he wanted her to know that she was beneath him and less than him so she was like, "Fuck that," and she uttered the hidden, unutterable name of God. And poof she went off flying and wouldn't come back. No matter how many angels God sent for her. She was like, "Fuck that, I will not lie under that douchebag."

LILIANA. Adam has always sounded very boring to me. Like he wouldn't be a very good dancer.

MARITZA. He didn't have to try too hard, did he? Everything was handed to him. He was a daddy's boy. Why would Lilith want to stay with him?

LILIANA. Well, he did come from a good family.

MARITZA. Adam was a pussy. He goes and whines to daddy about the wife situation so God – being the enabler that he is – gives Adam, Eve. Made from his rib and willing to be his little wifey and lie beneath him and have dinner for him on the table when he got home from doing nothing.

LILIANA. Poor Eve. Second wives always have it the worst.

> *(Beat.)*

Are we going to order room service?

MARITZA. There's no room service in motels, baby girl. I can go run and get you something.

LILIANA. Whataburger? Toasted bun.

MARITZA. You want Whataburger?

LILIANA. Yes. But in a little bit.

(They stare at each other a bit.)

So this is what you're making your art about? I mean, like your paintings.

MARITZA. Not just paintings. But yeah. Lilith is what I'm taking a look at next. Not just in paintings though. I'm starting to work with other materials.

LILIANA. Maritza. You're so smart. You're the smartest person I know.

MARITZA. I'm not smart.

LILIANA. *(Getting down from the dresser and onto the bed.)* No, you are. / You teach me things.

MARITZA. Whoa. Easy.

LILIANA. Can I like, make a hole on your head and put a straw in and suck out your smarts?

MARITZA. Ouch. That would hurt my head.

LILIANA. I mean, I'd leave you a little bit so you could finish your art stuff.

MARITZA. Well thank you.

*(**LILIANA** sucks on her ear playfully.)*

LILIANA. Here, give me some smarts, right now. / *(Nuzzling her ear.)*

…Come on, don't be stingy.

MARITZA. That's creepy, Lili. That's so creepy.

*(This whole thing builds into a pretty sweet but hot make out session. I mean, you let this go on for a while, okay? They end up tangled, **MARITZA** on top of **LILIANA**.)*

MARITZA. Run away with me.

LILIANA. Bite my toe. Here…bite my toe –

MARITZA. I'm dead serious.

LILIANA. Me too. Bite it.

MARITZA. I can't just leave you down here this time. I think you're going to go putrid, here.

LILIANA. Wilting flower. Me voy a churir.

MARITZA. I'm serious.

LILIANA. Wait, Changuita, *[little monkey]* Alberto is out of town. We have a whole day left. Ah, do you know what it's been here with you for two whole fucking days? I got freakin' bed sores and I love them. When do we just get to lie around and… Mari, please. Not yet. This is the best two days I've had in five years. Please, could we wait?

MARITZA. Why wait? I mean, let's just fast-forward to the end right now. / Let's spare us the –

LILIANA. *(Starts tugging on* MARITZA*'s jeans, trying to prevent her.)* No no no no…whatareyoudoing…nonono.

(She's got the jeans.)

Not yet. Please. Why do you want to put these on? Why are you trying to leave me?

MARITZA. Give me back my pants Liliana.

LILIANA. Why are you being like this? Qué mala eres. *[You are so bad.]*

MARITZA. Oh, I'm being bad?

LILIANA. See? You do understand Spanish. Cuando te conviene verdad… *[Only when it's convenient, right…]*

MARITZA. *(Trying to get her jeans back.)* Give me back my pants…

*(*LILIANA *sticks her fingers in her panties and* MARITZA *stops.* LILIANA *then sticks her wet fingers in* MARITZA*'s mouth.)*

Mala hierba. *[Bad seed/weed.]* See how bad you are?

LILIANA. Don't call me that. I hate it.

MARITZA. My mom was right. You're a bad seed.

*(*LILIANA *wraps herself in the sheet again.)*

LILIANA. Don't call me that. Why doesn't your mom like me? I hate that she never liked me.

MARITZA. Well, what do you think? Her daughter never moved on, walking around this world with a wire still stuck in your socket, / even one thousand miles away.

LILIANA. The way you say things…

MARITZA. It's true. I've been on pause for what? Seventeen years?

LILIANA. I don't want to talk about all this.

MARITZA. No, of course not.

LILIANA. Pinche choro mareador… *[Fucking broken record…]*

MARITZA. Fuck you, / I don't know what that means.

LILIANA. You always kill it. You kill the mood. / We're sitting here super nice talking about baby killers and the missionary position and you just have to go a tirarme tu pinche rollo que marea. *[with the same old fucking dizzying song]*

MARITZA. What is this to you? Wait, answer that. Why do I ask this every time? I ask this every fucking time and your answer breaks my heart every fucking time.

LILIANA. What do you want me to do?

MARITZA. You know what I want you to do.

LILIANA. You think this, between these four walls, you think this is real?

MARITZA. Do I think it's real or do I think it's sustainable?

LILIANA. What?

MARITZA. Do I think you'd come out of this room holding my hand? / No.

LILIANA. Oh, my God Maritza. ¡Claro que no! *[Of course not!]*

MARITZA. But do I think this is real? Do I think you've been in love with me since we were thirteen? Do I think I've been the ONE for you no matter what dudes have come in and out of your life? And do I think that you're too chicken-shit to do anything about it cuz you're too fucking hooked on being a fucking rich girl? Do I think that? Sure.

(Silence.)

LILIANA. Here are your jeans. Here. We should go, both of us.

*(**LILIANA** starts to look for her dress. She finds it and puts it on. Finds her panties and puts those on too. Now she looks for her shoes. **MARITZA** watches her do all this. Doesn't put on her jeans.)*

LILIANA. I can give you cash for… I can't use my card but I can give you cash.

(They stare at each other.)

Mari, you think I'm here…you think this doesn't cost me. You think it's just nothing. That you're nothing to me. To me you're actually…

(Beat.)

But everything costs. This is something I realized very early on. Everything has a price. And these two days with you, they're going to cost me big. But I don't care, I'll pay. Because it was so worth it.

MARITZA. What the fuck are you talking about?

(A moment.)

LILIANA. He is a monster. He likes choking. He likes belts. / He likes sticking things in places where they shouldn't be stuck. He's not a human to me sometimes. When he's grunting on top of me, or when he's ripping out my ass with no warning – because with Alberto, the more I scream the hotter he gets. But only if I mean it. No faking that shit…

MARITZA. Wait, what?
…Lili.

LILIANA. And that's the price. I pay for everything I own, Maritza. Everything I have. That car out there? Oh, I paid for that. With interest!

MARITZA. I think…you need…to stop telling me this or I'm going to go and kill this motherfucker.

LILIANA. No. Just…please, stop being in a fucking Antonio Banderas movie! Just. Stop. If you say something. If you do something, what will happen? He tosses me and my father's medical bills don't get paid. My mother loses her house, her health insurance too. My little sister has to come back from college and what? Wait tables? And me. I mean, what would happen to me? I have nothing. All I have is him.

    (Beat.)

We should go.

MARITZA. You can't keep paying for your sister's tuition with your body.

LILIANA. Okay, now you're calling me a hooker.

MARITZA. You're calling you a hooker.

LILIANA. It's so easy for you. You're free up there –

MARITZA. This is free?

LILIANA. You're up there, doing what you love. You can see who you want. You can go where you please. I got a family to feed, plus I'm not going to stand here and tell you that everything's all bad. Qué hipócrita sería. *[I'd be a hypocrite.]* So before you give me those googly-ass eyes, don't think that I got it so bad. Let's go, I want to go.

MARITZA. Why did you call me down here?

LILIANA. Because I'm a fucking idiot.

MARITZA. No, it's because you want to be with me. That's the truth of it.

LILIANA. God, don't you know that that is the only thing I think of sometimes. Forgetting everything and running to you? Not having to worry about my dad, my mom, my sister. Everybody.

MARITZA. Alright then. This time we make it happen. This time you come with me.

LILIANA. In what world are you living, Maritza?

MARITZA. He's out of town, we can do it before he comes back. We borrow a car from my cousin and we drive all the way up to Chicago.

LILIANA. He'll find me, Mari.

MARITZA. That's why we dismantle that narco truck of yours. Trade it with my cousin for parts so he can give us some hooptie that will take us north. It's not hard, Lili. He won't be able to track us. You just leave that iPhone here and take only what you need.

LILIANA. What do you mean only what I need?

MARITZA. Okay, you take whatever you want. Whatever we can fit in the back seat and in the trunk. Nothing electronic though, okay? No iPad. No laptop. No... whatever else you got. Just you and your drawers / and your face paint and your fancy shoes. But come on, not all of them, okay? And we go Liliana. We just start it. Take the video out of pause and finally press play. Like it was meant to be.

LILIANA. Mari.

MARITZA. This is a long time coming. Every so often we keep getting pulled back for a reason.

LILIANA. I know.

MARITZA. That's why you called me, Lili. And we are going to be fucked up unless we finally do this, we're never going to be whole. We'll walk around with big gaping holes for the rest of our lives.

(*Beat.*)

Please baby, you have to leave with me.

LILIANA. ...

(**LILIANA** *kisses* **MARITZA**.)

MARITZA. Tonight.

(*A pause while she waits for an answer.*)

Lili?

(Then **LILIANA** *kisses her back forcefully: It's a yes.)*

End of Scene

Scene Five

(Sunday Evening: The master bedroom. **LILIANA** *is packing. She does a little mad dance of "Should I take this? No. Yes, I need it," with almost everything she considers. After a while we hear a knock.)*

LILIANA. I'm taking a nap!

(More knocking.)

¿Quién es?!

YUYA. *(Offstage.)* Soy yo.

LILIANA. I'm taking a nap te digo. I'm napping! Go away.

YUYA. *(Offstage.)* Open the door.

LILIANA. Yuya, / respeta! I'm napping! Go away.

YUYA. *(Offstage.)* *(Some furious knocking.)* Open the door!

LILIANA. ¡Vete muchísimo a chingar a tu madre! Qué no te digo que estoy tomándome…

*(***YUYA*** has opened the door with her key. Fucking* **YUYA.***)*

Fucking Yuya. I fucking hate you.

YUYA. ¿Qué haces?

LILIANA. Te odio, ¿me oyes? / I fucking detest you.

YUYA. What are you doing? What are you doing?

LILIANA. What does it look like I'm doing? Close the fucking door at least.

(As she says this and **YUYA** *goes to close the door,* **FABIOLA** *enters the room in a freaking tornado of tears and* Housewives of The Rio Grande Valley *dramarama.)*

FABIOLA. …Aaaggrr…he's a fucking asshole! Mydad'samotherfuckingasshole! Oh, my God! I can't stand him! I can't fucking stand him. I want him to fucking fall off a cliff.

(Some crying. It's deep for **FABIOLA** *right now.)*

FABIOLA. I'm like completely... He's totally cut me off!

> (She holds out five credit cards. Gold, platinum...
> black.)

He canceled them all! My Saks card, my Macy's card.
He canceled... HE CANCELED MY NORDSTROM
CARD FOR FUCK'S SAKE. What am I going to have to
shop at fucking Old Navy now?!

> (Slight breakdown.)

My gas card. He canceled my motherfucking gas card!
You know what that means right? That I can't fucking
go anywhere. That means I'm trapped here.

YUYA. (To herself.) Ay no, Dios mío.

FABIOLA. What the fuck am I supposed to do with my
motherfucking life right now?!

LILIANA. What happened? Your dad's in Guadalajara. He's
not even...calm down Fabiola. Calmadita...when did
you talk to him? / Is he here?

FABIOLA. Yeah, on the phone just now. And now he hung
up on me and won't answer.

LILIANA. Fabiola, is he here?

FABIOLA. I want to kill myself right now.

LILIANA. Fabiola, what happened?

FABIOLA. He saw that I wasn't going to school.

LILIANA. He what?

FABIOLA. I haven't... I'm not in school right now. I just
needed some time to figure some stuff out... Hey, I
don't need the righteous shit right now, okay? I don't
need judgment right now, Liliana.

LILIANA. You haven't been going to school?

FABIOLA. No. But that's only because I didn't enroll,
okay? And the thing he doesn't see is that I made that
decision with like a clear adult mind. It wasn't like
my first two years where I had to drop out of classes
because I wasn't going, you know? Because I overslept
or because, well, most of my professors were total

douchebags. They didn't know what the hell they were talking about. Whatever. That's not even the... But why can't he see that this time, I made a conscious, responsible decision. To actually not waste money and time and whatever – aggravation. I consciously didn't enroll this semester. Alright, I didn't enroll this whole year. okay? I didn't enroll this year and well... He got all – Oh, God he scared the fuck out of me. He was like King Kong. You know how he gets like King Kong.

LILIANA. Yes.

FABIOLA. Yeah, but see he never gets like that with me.

LILIANA. I know.

FABIOLA. And he just...took it all away. He's never done that, Liliana. I'm like really scared right now because he's never done that. Even when I went to rehab for the... I mean he was like more caring than he was mad. Oh, my God I'm going to kill myself. That's what I'm going to tell him. That I'm going to kill myself. / See how he'd like his only daughter to...

LILIANA. Shh. Calm down, calm down, Fabi.

FABIOLA. Don't fucking tell me to calm down! Are you listening to me?!

LILIANA. Yes, I am listening to you.

FABIOLA. You have to talk to him.

(*Beat.*)

Liliana. You have to talk to him for me.

LILIANA. ...Ah, I think this is between you and him. Yo no me quiero meter.

FABIOLA. You have to help me! / I mean, what am I going to do? Live here like a prisoner? Like a slave? Just because he got into a mood?

LILIANA. Fabi, I don't want to get in the middle of...

FABIOLA. I need some cash.

LILIANA. If I take cash out right now, Fabiola...

FABIOLA. That's true. Who's to say he didn't cancel your shit too, right?

LILIANA. He wouldn't cancel my...

YUYA. You should check anyway.

LILIANA. Shh. Cierra el pico. I can't help you with actual money, Fabiola. I don't think he'd be very happy about that.

FABIOLA. Right. But if you –

(She heads to the jewelry boxes. Plural. There are a few.)

– gave me one of your little danglies here to sell, he wouldn't ever notice. Because why would he notice? / Or no, the really fancy stuff is in your closet, I know because I looked once. You have like fucking Cartier and Harry Winston shit. Oh, you have the Tiffany brooch he gave you the first year! The one with the big ruby.

*(**FABIOLA** has gone in the closet and hasn't stopped talking.)*

LILIANA. What! What are you...

FABIOLA. *(Offstage.)* It's in all these drawers right here, / I've seen them. I just need one of these and... Oh, my God. Is this a Chopard watch? Yes. Look at this thing! Why don't you ever wear this? Fuck me. David Yurman bracelets are worth nothing right? They won't give me shit for these. Where are your earrings?

YUYA. *(The following four lines overlap with **FABIOLA**'s closet monologue.)* You're just going to let her?

LILIANA. What do you want me to do?

YUYA. You can't just let her.

LILIANA. What do you want me to do? Little fucking bitch.

YUYA. You're going to let her clean you out like that?

*(**FABIOLA** emerges with a ton of things and the brooch.)*

FABIOLA. Found the brooch. This thing's huge and tacky. You don't want to wear this.

LILIANA. Fabiola, mi vida, could you sit down so we can –

FABIOLA. Do you have earrings?

LILIANA. ...you can't take those things.

FABIOLA. He's not even going to notice.

LILIANA. No, you can't take those things because they're mine.

FABIOLA. Liliana, I like you but I don't want to say something offensive to you, okay?

(Moves to go.)

LILIANA. You're not going anywhere with those. Those are my things.

FABIOLA. Excuse me, but nothing in this house is yours, okay? You're here on lease. Don't start getting any ideas and DON'T start getting comfortable, honey. / You got a shelf life of about...

LILIANA. *(She snatches the shit.* **FABIOLA** *puts up a little fight but loses.)* Well, HONEY, until he sends me away, these are my things. And you're a spoiled little bitch to come in here and think you can just take my stuff. Do you hear that? Who raised you?

FABIOLA. Are you serious right now?

LILIANA. Dead serious. Who fucking raised you? Wolves?

(Pause.)

FABIOLA. I'm calling my father and telling him exactly what kind of a gold digger he brought into our house.

LILIANA. Do it. Maybe he'll answer the phone.

FABIOLA. Fuck you.

LILIANA. Come on. Call him. Oh, wait. Did he cut off your phone too?

FABIOLA. Fuck you, you tacky bitch.

(Storming off, she bumps into **YUYA.***)*

Get out of my fucking way you fucking idiot!

(She exits. Good riddance.)

(Door slam. **YUYA** *and* **LILIANA** *are a little stunned. A moment. Oh, shit.)*

YUYA. Si se contenta con su Papá – It won't be pretty if she get's her daddy's ear again.

LILIANA. I KNOW! Don't you know I know that blood is blood.

It doesn't matter though. That doesn't matter anymore.

(She starts to pull herself together and resumes the packing.)

I don't give a fuck. Fuck that little bratty bitch. And fuck Alberto. I don't care anymore. What can he do to me now, huh?

*(**YUYA** is staring at **LILIANA**. It's unnerving.)*

WHAT? What is this face? What!

YUYA. How many years and I've kept my mouth shut? Not one word. And don't think I don't know the cochinadas you do with her. Doing disgusting things with your bodies – the two of you. Sucias.

LILIANA. Cállate pendeja.

YUYA. Liliana, you know you can't leave with her. What, you would leave your father, the way he is right now? So sick? / You would leave your pobre mamacita? That poor woman. / You think you get to run off with that puta in your happily ever after and not think about anyone but yourself? Mi'ja, what will happen to your family, then? You know Alberto will cut them all off.

LILIANA. / Shut up. Cállate Yuya. Shutthefuckup! Shut the fuck up hija de tu puta madre! Shutthefuckup…shut up Yuya…

*(**LILIANA** has rushed to **YUYA** in a fury. She is beating her back, her arms. **YUYA** cowers and covers her face, and takes the blows. **LILIANA** lets it all go. They both end up on the floor. The hitting becomes an embrace of sorts.)*

Don't say these things to me, Yuya.

YUYA. You can't go anywhere. Too many of us depend on you. Who knows how long this guy will keep you around but in the meantime, you have to be a smart girl y aprovechar.

(Quick beat.)

Man, if I had your possibilities, I would not be fucking this up. I'd be saving every penny I could. Hiding shit. Stashing it away. You need to get smarter about this, Lili. And then, when it's done, then maybe you can think of…maybe you can think of whatever cochinadas you want to think about. When you've squeezed everything you can out of this whole thing. Es un investment. Are you listening to me?

(Takes **LILIANA**'s *face, both still on the floor.)*

This is all an investment. But you gotta buck up. Be a mujercita. You think I don't want to go off, galavanting and… I don't know. You think I like being for your every whim? I didn't say when I was a baby girl, a mira, that's what I want to do with my life. Live at the whims of those who have more. But I got people who are counting on me and I'm the only thing they got. And your Papi and your Mami, tu hermana Cecilia, you're the only thing they got. It's not about you, it's about them. So buck up.

(She untangles herself and stands up.)

You listening? You're gonna have to buck the fuck up.

(She exits.)

End of Scene

Scene Six

(Late Sunday: Outskirts of McAllen. One of those side roads off of another side road made of dirt. **MARITZA** *is sitting on a rock. The headlights from an old car are her only light source. She's pacing. Making plans. A while before we hear the crackle of tires on the dirt.* **LILIANA** *gets out of her Expedition and* **MARITZA** *is activated; she's a galvanized girl right now. She's on go.)*

MARITZA. See? I told you that it would take no time at all. Nolana and then to the highway. / It's actually easy to get to, right?

LILIANA. Yeah, no…it wasn't hard.

MARITZA. The iPhone. You left that iPhone at home right? They can track it.

*(**LILIANA** nods.)*

And the GPS. You didn't use the GPS right? I mean, you kind of didn't need it the way I told you to come.

LILIANA. No, I didn't use the GPS.

MARITZA. Good. That's good, baby.

LILIANA. I hate that thing anyway. That woman always sounds like she's mocking me. "Turn left here." Fuck you! YOU turn left here.

MARITZA. Is this bag all you got? / We should switch out your bags and put them in my car.

LILIANA. What? No, of course not. Do you expect me to shove the contents of my entire – This is a purse! This is a purse, Maritza.

(It's kind of big for a purse, but whatever. You could fit a head in there.)

MARITZA. Yes. I'm sorry, this is a purse.

*(**MARITZA** holds **LILIANA** by the arms. She stares deep into her. Checks her to see if she's alright. Kisses her maybe. **LILIANA** lets her.)*

MARITZA. Hey.

>   *(Pause.)*

Hey.

>   *(Beat.)*

How are you doing, baby?

LILIANA. I think I have to pee.

MARITZA. There's a gas station. We can stop there / before…

LILIANA. Do you live in a two flat?

MARITZA. Do I what?

LILIANA. Do you live in a two flat. And what IS a two flat, for that matter? I've heard people in big cities say they live on two flats and actually to me, that sounds very uncomfortable.

MARITZA. What, like a condo? Like a split home?

LILIANA. What's a split home?! A split home sounds even worse than a two flat. I don't… Maritza, do you split your home?

MARITZA. Are you asking if I have a roommate? I don't have a roommate.

LILIANA. What kind of a house do you have?

MARITZA. I don't have a house. You know that. People in Chicago don't have houses, Lili. Well, not like the houses you're used to. I have an apartment. And not like the apartment where your sister lives that is basically a townhome. Okay. Liliana what's with the questions?

LILIANA. So nobody has a house in the entire city of Chicago?

MARITZA. Some people do.

LILIANA. Some? Which people? How do people have kids?! Where do people put their kids?

MARITZA. Where do people *put* their kids?

LILIANA. O sea, I find it hard to believe that a family with three kids lives in an apartment. That's something I find very hard to understand.

MARITZA. *(Really trying hard not to lose her patience.)* Well, yes, actually, families with three kids do live in apartments but also people who need more room move to the suburbs. If space happens to be an issue.

LILIANA. Would we live in the suburbs if we needed more room?

MARITZA. No, I'd rather stab myself in the eye than live in the suburbs! Where the fuck is all this coming from? Why would we need more room? What, are we thinking of having kids now? Is that what we're doing?

LILIANA. Well, are we? Those are questions, right?

>   *(Beat.)*

In your life, do you ever want kids, Maritza?

MARITZA. Um, you know what I want? I want to get going. I want to get on the road, put some distance between McAllen and us and when we get to like, I don't know, Austin or Dallas then I can talk about kids, or getting a pet or whatever else you want. / Right now I want to get on the road.

LILIANA. Kids are not pets.

MARITZA. I know kids are not pets.

LILIANA. You don't want kids either, do you? Alberto doesn't want kids. That was one of his conditions. I want kids. I want kids really bad. What's the point if there are no kids, you know? What's the point? God, I've never said that out loud.

MARITZA. All of this. I mean, ALL of it, baby, we will sit down and talk about. I want to spend days and days just talking about this kind of shit. Imagining this life and that life. I can't fucking wait. But right now, I want you in that truck, I want to drop it off where my cousin told me to drop it off and I want to get the fuck out of the valley. Now can you please get your ass in that truck? Liliana.

(LILIANA's, like, on another planet.)

LILIANA. It was like a diamond heist getting out of the house. You know what you forgot to think about? The cameras. We have a million cameras. But don't worry, I thought of the cameras. I thought about everything. I said, I'll pack my life in those suitcases and think about everything. The cold. The stairs. What kind of shoes will be good for the subway, because you're making me go on the subway, right? / That's the kind of thing I'm signing up for. Hey, I like the subway. I've been on the Underground. I rode around in that.

MARITZA. The EL. Yeah, you're going to have to take the EL, Liliana. It's not a fucking tragedy that your ass will have to get on the bus once in a while.

LILIANA. Wait, what? What did you say? It's not a fucking tragedy? To you maybe it's not a fucking tragedy but what am I going to do up there? Nunca he conocido a un negro, ¡Maritza! I've never in my life had a conversation with a black person? What will I say?

MARITZA. Alright, youknowwhat –

LILIANA. I won't know what to say to them.

MARITZA. Alright, you're going to have to not say racist shit like / that when we're up there, Liliana. We're going to have to re-train that fucking xenophobic mind of yours.

LILIANA. Why is that racist? It's true!

(Beat.)

Re-train? Like I'm a doggie?

MARITZA. I didn't mean like a dog. / Come on, Liliana. Jesus, come on.

LILIANA. Because I'm a little animalito to be trained? Because I'm a little idiot who didn't go to college to learn words like xenophobic. For your information, I know what xenophobic means. Para que lo sepas. Everybody always thinking I'm so stupid.

MARITZA. Who's thinking you're stupid? Baby, I don't think you're stupid. Lili, please. You're picking a fight right now. / You're afraid of this trip and you're picking a...

LILIANA. Don't tell me what I'm doing! Plus we're not just taking a *trip*, Maritza. Para ti está facilito, ¿no? / I'm about to flip myself upside down, but to you it's just a trip.

MARITZA. Alright, you're right. Not just a trip.

LILIANA. This is the – no, / listen to me. ¡Cállate! Listen to me. Logistics. You and I didn't talk about the logistics. What's so bad that I want to talk about the pinche logistics, huh? What's so wrong with that?

MARITZA. But baby... We have to...

What logistics?

(An "oh fuck" beat.)

Liliana. Do you have bags in that truck?

(Beat.)

Are there suitcases in that truck? Are you coming with me, Liliana?

LILIANA. My father. In all of this never have you mentioned what we're going to do about my father. My sister. How come you haven't brought that up? You haven't talked about anything but Chicago, but here. The life I'm leaving here, you haven't mentioned that once. What the fuck am I going to do about... I don't know, my friends. I'm leaving all my friends!

MARITZA. Those people aren't your friends, Lili.

LILIANA. I know you don't think so but I do have friends, Mari. I have good friends here.

MARITZA. Fake-ass people that greet you with a kiss on the cheek and a stab in the back.

LILIANA. What do you know about my life?

MARITZA. What?

LILIANA. What do you know about my life anymore? En serio. What do you know about what my life is now?

MARITZA. You're serious?

LILIANA. Look, I have a life here. / Que a ti no te guste es otra cosa. *[That you don't like it is another matter altogether.]* But I like a lot of my life here and that's what you will never understand. I like walking into a restaurant and seeing people gasp. I like to hear them whispering. Them whispering in that good way.

MARITZA. Wait, what are we talking about right now? What are you saying?

They're not whispering in the good way. They are measuring you up and down, Liliana.

LILIANA. What! I like that. You don't get that I like that. I like being recognized. I like it when Alberto and I make our appearance. I know that's stupid to you, pero a mi me gusta que me envidien. *[I like to be envied]* For so long I had nothing. Nothing, Maritza. And now look at me. Oh, you don't get it. You don't get that it's not all so bad. That man saved our life. What would we have done? My family would be on the street. I'd be working at Sally's Beauty Supply or something. On welfare... who knows. I don't want to think about it.

MARITZA. What are you saying right now, Lili?

LILIANA. Nothing. I'm not saying anything. Just that it's kind of hard to be told your life is shit. My whole life is not shit. I'm not...shit...

> (**LILIANA** *breaks down. Like falls to the ground and shit.* **MARITZA** *is on her, kissing her, trying to hold her.* **LILIANA** *pulls away but* **MARITZA**'s *clasp is strong.* **LILIANA** *finally gives in.*)

MARITZA. I'm sorry if I made this sound easy. Shhh. It's not easy. Oh, you're shaking. Nonono, no shaking Mamá. You don't have to be scared anymore.

> *(Kisses.)*

It's all done. Tonight, that's all over and done with. In a day we'll be in St. Louis at my brother's and then, two days, tops, we'll be in the Chi. Just you and me in

Chicago. You know the first thing I'm gonna do for you when we get home? I'm going to run you a bath. You loved baths, right? Well, I have a big old bathtub.

LILIANA. I'll turn into a raisin.

MARITZA. Yeah, a big old sexy fucking raisin. And then, when you've gotten your fill of baths and sleeping and whatever the fuck. Then you go do you. You go do what you got to do for you. I mean, what you were always meant to do before the money problems and this motherfucker got a hold of you. You can just be you.

LILIANA. Who the fuck is that?

MARITZA. No. I know you. You're in there, you're somewhere in there under all this shit on your face, under this weave.

LILIANA. It's not a weave. Son extensiones. [They're extensions.]

MARITZA. Denial.

LILIANA. Hey, this is Indian hair. It cost me twelve hundred dollars.

MARITZA. Oh, is that right? Well, let's me and you and your Indian weave get out of here so we can get going. Plus your skirt's going to get dirty sitting there on the ground like that.

LILIANA. The ground is so dry here. You know, you never think about that… You never touch the ground. So rocky…

MARITZA. You don't care if you get all dirty?

LILIANA. I never just sit like this.

MARITZA. I know. You're going to rip your tight ass skirt. You okay?

LILIANA. (Nods.) Look at this big old rock…

(She's been fingering a rock, she picks it up. It's heavy on her hand.)

MARITZA. You know, I like you a little dirty. When you're just you. When you don't give a fuck. I like it when you get whispies like this, these little strands. I like it when they fly away. When your makeup rubs off, when I see your real lips without all the sticky shit.

LILIANA. Eres una pinche hippie. *[You're a fucking hippie.]*

MARITZA. I like the color of your lips. They don't make that color in a lipstick. I love your lips.

> *(Kisses and kisses and maybe, if it's not too much, more kisses. They're both tangled on the ground. A long pause as they size each other up.* **MARITZA** *stands up.* **LILIANA** *is going to do something. There's a moment, a good moment there, and then* **LILIANA***'s iPhone rings.* **MARITZA***'s mood changes. She sees that it's not her phone.)*

MARITZA. That's not my phone.

> *(Beat.)*

Why is your iPhone ringing?

LILIANA. I thought I left it at home.

MARITZA. Did you?

LILIANA. Es Alberto.

MARITZA. I told you to not bring that shit with you.

LILIANA. What am I going to do? Not have a phone?

MARITZA. You're not thinking of answering that shit, are you?

LILIANA. I have to answer it, Maritza.

MARITZA. Don't fucking –

LILIANA. *(Answers that shit.)* ¿Bueno? Hola mi amor. / ¿Qué pasó mi rey? *[Hello? Hi sweetheart. What's going on, dear?]* Already? I thought you were coming back on Tuesday – you're here now?

> *(To* **MARITZA***.)*

Fuck he's here.

> *(To Alberto.)*

Sí mi amor. *[Yes, of course.]*

MARITZA. Oh God, I'm gonna hurl...you had to bring your fucking piece of shit iPhone.

LILIANA. ¿Cómo? Eh, sí no…es que ando aquí con una amiga. *[Excuse me? Eh, yes no… I'm here with a friend.]*

>   *(Beat.)*

Just a friend. We're just having coffee –

>   *(Beat.)*

Sí – Sí, nada más termino aquí y voy directito para la casa – *[Yes – yes, as soon as I finish here and I'll head straight home.]*

>   *(MARITZA yanks the phone from LILIANA and hangs up.)*

MARITZA! Me va a matar. *[He's going to kill me.]* You can't just hang up on him. Give me the phone. Maritza. Give me the phone.

>   *(The following is a messy game of "keep away," MARITZA gets a little rough at pushing LILIANA away, but LILIANA keeps hurling herself at her trying to get the damn iPhone.)*

MARITZA. Do you even have bags in the car?

LILIANA. Of course I have bags in the car. I HAVE TWO FUCKING BAGS IN THAT TRUCK WHICH NOW HOLD EVERYTHING I HAVE IN THE WORLD.

>   *(MARITZA's holding the phone above her head. LILIANA lunges for it again.)*

Puta madre, ¡dáme el pinche teléfono! *[Fucking shit, give me the motherfucking phone!]* I have to call him back!

MARITZA. Fuck you, you mala hierba.

LILIANA. *(She's a hot mess for real now.)* Please Mari.

MARITZA. Fuck you and your tears, fucking actress. You had me do this whole fucking thing –

LILIANA. We'll talk in two seconds, just please… Mari, let me call him back. I'm not doing this to be…you are not understanding, he'll be so pissed. He'll get like a maniac. / OhGodOhGod. He probably came back early to deal with fucking Fabi. Maritza, please!

(She's bawling by now.)

Mari, please...

MARITZA. You were never coming to Chicago. Why would you bring this phone? GOD! And I'm a fucking dumbass who runs around making this whole elaborate plan – Fuck... My mom always warns me too. "Es mala hierba. She'll break your heart or worse."

LILIANA. Mari please... / you don't know what will happen...

MARITZA. She kept telling me. "She's bad news."

(The phone rings again. They freeze.)

LILIANA. Maritza, he will kill us! /

(Dives for the phone.)

Dáme el teléfono por favor. *[Give me the phone please.]*

MARITZA. Get the fuck away from me...

(They start being a little too rough with each other over this fucking phone.)

LILIANA. I'M NOT PLAYING, I NEED TO ANSWER! DÁME EL PINCHE TELÉFONO – *[Give me the fucking phone –]*

MARITZA. You know what? You're right, somebody should answer this motherfucking phone.

LILIANA. Maritza...

MARITZA. *(Answers it.)* Hello?

LILIANA. NO!

*(The following is even messier. **LILIANA** lunges for the phone as **MARITZA** tries to remain on it. They struggle. **MARITZA** drops the phone and dives to get it. She gives **LILIANA** a giant kick that sends her flying to the ground. **LILIANA** almost hits her head against that big ass rock she was playing with. Ugh. Why are they being a Latina Lesbian stereotype right now? **MARITZA** puts the stupid phone to her ear and speaks.)*

MARITZA. Hey...hey, sorry about that. Sorry, my man. What's up Alberto? How are things, my friend? Hey, I meant to tell you, nice party the other night. Loved the band. Classy stuff.

> *(Beat.)*

Ah, funny you should ask that, funny story. You see, I'm a friend of your wife's. Actually, very good friend, you stupid fuck! Let me tell you a little fucking story about destiny and about –

> *(**LILIANA**'s gotten up in a flash and in her panic, she's picked up that rock she was playing with earlier. That fucking thing is heavy as hell but before she has a chance to think, she rushes to **MARITZA** and raises it over her head to hit **MARITZA** in the back of the head! But right before we see the blow:)*

> *(Blackout.)*

Oh, shit.

End of Scene

Scene Seven

(Sunday Night: LILIANA, face scrubbed clean and wearing a messy ponytail, stands like a statue staring into the eerie light of the pool. From inside the house you can hear Alberto shouting something and FABIOLA replying with loud whimpers. We can't really understand what the fight is about, but we can tell someone is very angry. After a bit, YUYA enters. She lights a cigarette and takes a drag. After a beat she notices LILIANA standing by the pool.)

YUYA. No asustes. *[Don't scare people.]*

  (Beat.)

I knew you'd come back.

LILIANA. *(Still looking at the pool.)* I came back.

YUYA. I know. That's good. That's real good, Lili.

LILIANA. I came back.

  (A pause. We can hear the fight going on inside.)

YUYA. Don't even think about going in there. Es Armaggedon up in there. Book of Revelations. Pinche huerca's in there pleading her case.

LILIANA. He'll get over it.

YUYA. I don't know if her tears will work this time, I watched him go in el study; red steam was coming out de sus ears.

  (Beat.)

Whatsu matter? You sad?

LILIANA. Am I sad…?

YUYA. Yo sabía que you'd come back. You did the right thing, mi'ja.

  (Pause. Some more shouting from inside.)

What happened to your face?

LILIANA. *(Suddenly a slight worry.)* Why, do I have something on my face?

YUYA. Well, no tienes makeup on.

LILIANA. Oh.

>   *(Beat.)*

I had to scrub it all off.

YUYA. Why are you all...looking like that? With your hair like that? Ah, ya sé. A last hurrah before you sent her off? Ey, whatever you had to do. S'long as you got rid of her. However you had to say your goodbyes. Because, chulita, you got some shit to worry about in that house.

>   *(Beat.)*

Wait. You sent her away, right? Liliana, did you send her away?

LILIANA. She's gone.

YUYA. A qué bueno.

LILIANA. And I came back. *(Beat.)* Because this is what I chose, right?

YUYA. Si, mi'ja.

LILIANA. *(Finally animating.)* Yuya, do you know the story of Lilith?

YUYA. De who?

LILIANA. She was a wife first and then, because she didn't do what she was told, she became a demon. But I know she was no demon. It's just what people say. People like to say awful things. People call you things, when you're little, they say things because maybe your dad doesn't have money and he owes people and you show up with torn shoes and all the girls in school, they...they say mean things. They say mean things about your family. They call you names. But you're not a mala hierba. You're not. You're not a demon.

>   *(Beat.)*

Poor Lilith. She had to grow those talons to claw her way out. I understand her.

YUYA. Te estás freakiando, Lily? You want me to get you a Tafil to calm down?

LILIANA. I'm no demon, Yuya.

YUYA. Stop saying demon, it's freaking me out. You want a pill?

LILIANA. Tell me I'm no demon.

(Beat.)

YUYA. Ey. Whatever you got going on, todo tus feelings, you gotta know it's worth it because this whole thing? All this? It takes work. And you puttin' in the work, mi'ja. You're good at this. At this wife thing.

LILIANA. Yes, I am. I can be Eve and lie beneath him.

YUYA. Yeah, you do what you got to do. Convince him now for a baby and you will be golden.

LILIANA. You think he would let me keep a baby this time?

YUYA. There are ways. But you have to do something with that face and just, put yourself together.

LILIANA. I want babies, Yuya. Lots of them.

*(Abruptly and out of freakin' nowhere, **FABIOLA** and her puffy, wet face enter through the patio doors.)*

FABIOLA. Great. Fucking great.

(She starts to go back inside.)

Is there nowhere to go in this fucking house!

LILIANA. Fabiola, wait.

FABIOLA. What. Seriously, what. I really don't feel like fighting with you right now.

LILIANA. I don't want to fight with you either.

FABIOLA. Oh, please.

LILIANA. I don't.

FABIOLA. Listen, you win it all, okay ay? You win.

LILIANA. You think somebody wins here? Nobody ever wins.

FABIOLA. All I know is that ever since you came to our house Dad has been completely different. He would have never, I mean never screamed at me like he just screamed at me. You totally turned him against me.

LILIANA. You think I did that?

FABIOLA. Of course.

　　　(Beat.)

Not that you give a fuck, but he's the only person I have left in the world. You swooped in here and poisoned him. He wants nothing to do with me. He just told me. You don't know what that feels like. To have absolutely no one.

　　　(A silence while **FABIOLA** *cries.* **LILIANA** *slowly gets up.* **YUYA'***s just in the corner, observing.)*

LILIANA. What did he say to you? What exactly did he say to you?

FABIOLA. What *didn't* he say to me…

LILIANA. What was the last thing he said? Does he want you to leave? Is he going to help you anymore?

FABIOLA. You-know-what-Liliana…!

LILIANA. I'm trying to help you.

　　　(Beat.)

What did he say?

FABIOLA. That I'm out of chances.

LILIANA. You're not out of chances.

　　　(Beat.)

Are you hungry?

FABIOLA. What?

　　　(It's as if **LILIANA***'s wings expand throughout the following…)*

LILIANA. Fabi, you're going to go inside with Yuya. She's going to make you dinner, because I'm almost positive you haven't eaten. Yuya, you're going to make her dinner. Whatever she wants. You figure it out. And I'm going to go, I'm going to go talk to your dad. And then you're going to talk to him again. And apologize.

Without all this. Like a grown-up. And tomorrow you're going to go back up to Houston. With his support. And you're going to go back to school, and stay out of trouble. You will stay out of trouble, okay ay. And you and me, Fabi, you and me we are going to have an understanding.

>	*(Beat.)*

Do we have an understanding?

FABIOLA. What?

LILIANA. Do we have an understanding?

FABIOLA. I don't even know what you're…

>	*(Beat.)*

Yeah. We have an understanding.

>	**(LILIANA** *takes out a makeup compact from her purse.)*

LILIANA. Good. Yuya. Take her inside and make her some dinner.

>	**(LILIANA** *starts applying makeup.)*

Go on. Anda, ve con Yuya. I'll be in to talk to your dad in just a minute. Don't you worry about a thing.

YUYA. *(To* **FABIOLA.***)* Do you want your Eggs Benedict?

FABIOLA. What? No. Just…whatever. Just make me whatever. Thank you.

YUYA. Buena pues.

>	**(YUYA** *goes inside and* **FABIOLA** *follows* **LILIANA.***)*
>	*(Stopping her.)*

FABIOLA. We're not going to worry about a thing.

>	*(They exit.)*

>	**(LILIANA** *slowly applies blush. This is a meticulous ritual. Something happens to her before our eyes. A hardening? Carefully, she takes out a blood-red lipstick from her purse and applies it like a neurosurgeon. She stares into the compact as if she's*

lost something. Nope. It's all still there. But better.
Her attention turns to the bag. She contemplates
it for a moment, then she grabs it and stands up.
She heads toward the patio doors and right before
she's going to go inside, **LILIANA** *pulls down her*
gorgeous hair from that ponytail and fluffs it up.
In she goes.)

(Mala hierba.)

Fin